Adven.

Number Eighteen

Sharon Lee and Steve Miller

Pinbeam Books
http://www.pinbeambooks.com

Copyright Page
Courier Run

"Kin Ties," First published by the authors on Splinter Universe (http://www.splinteruniverse.com), July 2011

"Guaranteed Delivery," First published by the authors on Splinter Universe (http://www.splinteruniverse.com), September 2011

ISBN:978-1-948465-02-1
Published December 2011 by
Pinbeam Books
PO Box 1586
Waterville ME 04903
email info@pinbeambooks.com
Cover Copyright © December 18, 2011
Cover design by Steve Miller

Guaranteed Delivery

Light bloomed inside the treasure room.

Discreet and faintly blue, it kissed the alarm console, the pearly security keys blushing delft.

Long fingers touched the shy panels, pressing them in a precise, rapid sequence. More light bloomed, opening a path across the carpet to a wall well-hung with twodee art.

The owner of those long, sure fingers, one Dollance-Marie Chimra, upon whom the Feinik society news had bestowed the name Alabaster, kept scrupulously to the illuminated path. As she approached the wall, light began to glow in outline around a single piece of art—a painting of a woman in long skirts, the shawl covering her hair framing a face ferocious with love, one arm around the waist of a man in a tattered uniform, braced on a crude crutch.

"Treasure of the House," was the name of the painting; the original hung in the salon of Dollance-Marie's mama, the Gransella of Hamptonshire, seated on Albion itself.

Dollance-Marie pressed her right thumb against a particular point in the painting's plain wood frame, counted to ten, then folded both hands at her waist, waiting.

Silent on stealth hinges, the painting swung away from the wall, revealing a door, and a simple tumbler lock.

It required only a moment for her to work the combination, pull the door open, and remove a plain velvet box slightly smaller than her palm.

She paused, long fingers curled into a cage around the box. Had it been someone other than Dollance-Marie Chimra, and had there been anyone in the treasure room to see, that hidden watcher might have said that she...hesitated.

As it was Alabaster herself, whom the tabloids had in their genius named well, and no one else inside the tightly-guarded room—she paused, only that, and took a deep, cleansing breath before she closed the safe and spun the tumblers. The painting swung back into place, light fading from its perimeter.

Raising her chin, Alabaster met the fierce eyes of the woman in the frame, and smiled.

#

She had planned the evening carefully—first, drinks in Erabeck's public parlor, to satisfy those who followed Alabaster; then befores with Smyth-Erin Nodmere and Dane Belnesky—Yin and Yang, according to the society news, in recognition of their long and complimentary partnership.

From Yin and Yang's semi-public table, they proceeded to a private dining nook, said privacy Erabeck's specific guarantee.

The door closed behind the security escort. Dollance-Marie put her palm against the plate. The room chimed, indicating that the privacy blanket was in force.

She turned with a smile that had no place on Alabaster's face, and stepped forward to seat her guest.

"Please," she said, moving the chair on its track, "be comfortable."

John Vernon tipped his head, considering her from serious blue eyes.

"Must we be formal?" he asked, and she paused with her hand on the back of the chair.

Vernon was a good bloodline, if not so exalted as Chimra. The family elders had collected a following of note, which they managed with a subtlety even Chimra might with profit study.

This particular Vernon, whom the media had ignored until Alabaster had engaged him for a moment of conversation—this John Vernon, now code-named Galahad, had been raised out of society by his father's people on Hascove, this having been stipulated in the Terms of Dissolution. He had returned, unRanked and with a scant base of Followers, to his mother's house and business upon achieving his majority—also in accordance with the Terms. He possessed a lively wit and was quick to learn—so quick that one sometimes forgot that he *was* learning, until he asked just such a sweet, naive question.

"We are private," Dollance-Marie said, matching him for seriousness,"and may be as informal as you wish."

As soon as she had uttered the words, with their suggestion of more risque ventures, she wished to call them back. Others that she had favored with her notice would have immediately heard an invitation to sport, and acted accordingly.

John, raised in innocence, only smiled, his sweet countenance undisturbed by even a blush. He settled with casual elegance into the seat she held for him, touching one finger to the seal at his throat, loosening it somewhat.

Taking her own seat, Dollance-Marie smiled. John's dislike of the current male fashion for tight collars and flowing tunics was his mother's despair.

"Perhaps we ought to have you establish a fashion for neck scarves," she said, pouring wine into painted palm-cups.

"And be choked twice?" he asked.

She leaned forward and offered him a cup, which he took with a frank smile.

"How if," she mused,"the vogue was to drape the scarf loosely in order to call attention to a charming dishevelment?"

"My mother would murder me."

She laughed, and brought her cup against his.

"To informality," she said.

"To informality, and all its pleasures," he answered, capping her, according to the latest mode.

Dollance-Marie gave him a sharp glance.

"Is something wrong?" he asked, alert, as ever, to her moods.

Alabaster would have answered that question with her cool, cutting laugh. Dollance-Marie smiled a small smile.

"You've been studying again," she said."That was quite fashionable."

Such notice of his progress might have pleased any another country cousin striving to learn greatness. John...frowned, and put his cup aside, untasted.

"I have been studying," he said slowly."I must, for my mother has set me to learn so that I can take my place in the family business. But I am determined not to be *fashionable* with my true friends, Marie. I beg your pardon."

True friends was a notion from backward Hascove. That it had survived John's first year moving in the Leadership levels of Feinik society was a testament to its tenacity. Or, as certain of Alabaster's acquaintence might say, John's lack of motherwit.

Dollance-Marie knew that John's wits lacked nothing. And she had admitted to her innermost self that she was charmed—no! that she was *honored*, to employ another little-used phrase of the Leaders—to be one of his *true friends*.

Her breath caught on that thought, and her heart took up the odd pounding that John's presence had lately woken. It was, she thought, time. She had done her research; she had formally expressed her intentions to her mama, who had, depend upon it, done *her* research, and had raised no protest. John Vernon had captured her attention; he was comely, sweet, and modest. His father's people had kept him close, so Dollance-Marie need not be concerned with paying off any of his wildoats, or placating a former liaison.

She would be his first—*that* was a thought that warmed her blood distractingly during her precious hours of privacy. She would teach him—so very many things.

Her hand shook; the wine in the palm-cup shivered.

"Marie?" He touched her wrist gently."Is something wrong?"

It was time. Now. She *must* have him.

"Not wrong," she said. Putting her cup aside, and reaching to take his hand between both of hers."John, I—I propose that we two come to an agreement of partnership."

He blinked.

"Partnership?" he repeated."Like Dane and Erin?"

Yin and Yang had renewed their agreement more times than Dollance-Marie could count. She shivered at the thought of entering into so long a partnership—but of course John hadn't meant to imply such a thing; it was his innocence speaking again.

"Like Erin and Dane," she agreed, therefore, and smiled at him, while her heart pounded against her ribs, and her breath came short.

"I know," she said."I know that it must seem very sudden to you. You mustn't be frightened, or think that I will be angry if you want time to think, or—" But no; she was not going to put the unthinkable into his sweet, naive head. She was not going to lose him. And while she might be his *true friend*, she doubted not at all the necessity of what she did next. Hadn't her grandmama taught her? *Pay good value for what you want.*

She kept hold of John with one hand; with the other, she reached into her pocket for the velvet box. Gently, she placed it on the table before him, and tapped it so that the lid rose, revealing a faceted ruby the size of her thumb, from nail to knuckle. The storied Hampton-shire Ruby. She felt a small tremor, looking at it—not *exactly* hers to give, but a treasure of the house. As John would be.

"That," she said softly, "is yours."

John glanced down, and blinked, likely dazzled, as were most when they first beheld the Ruby. He raised his head to look directly into her eyes.

"Marie, are you certain?"

She blinked in her turn.

"Certain?" she repeated, noticing then that it was now her hand held with firm sweetness between his two palms.

"I can think of nothing better than...than a partnership with my true friend," John said seriously. "But..." His lips twisted into a wry smile. "I *have* been learning, and I know that my view of the matter is not...current here on Feinik."

"I can think of nothing that I want more than for us to be togeth-er, in public and in private," Dollance-Marie said truthfully. Right now, she wanted John with her; she would, she thought, take ill if she could not have him.

John nodded. "Then I accept. I think that the traditional initial term is one planetary year?"

"Yes," she said eagerly. "I'll send my formal request to your mother this evening. And the Ruby—I'll have it made into a ring for you, John. Will you like that?"

He frowned, almost as if he had forgotten all about the magnifi-cent gem she had given him.

"If it pleases you," he answered.

***

The comm light was dark.

"Oh," said Aelliana, leathered shoulders drooping. She put her hand on the back of the pilot's chair, frowning at the board as if the application of raw will would produce a message in queue.

Daav, who had come onto the bridge in her wake, paused at her shoulder, and waited a decent count of twelve before clearing his throat.

"As eager to lift as that, Pilot?"

"Well..." She sighed and turned to him, her eyes wide and very green."One does wish for work, after all. We have put our name and our credentials on the for-hire lists, and I had thought, that, surely..."

Her voice faded.

"You had thought that surely, *Ride the Luck*, with three successful contracts fulfilled, would speedily attract not one, but several job offers," he finished for her.

"If you will have it," Aelliana said steadily."Ridiculous it may be, but a pilot has a certain pride in her ship, and in the abilities of herself *and* her copilot, sad rogue that he otherwise stands."

"*That's* set me in place!"

"Yes; as it should." She sighed, and continued more seriously."Truly, Daav, if we are to continue this course we have chosen—and perhaps someday see profit from it!—we cannot lift empty."

"Indeed, we cannot," he agreed, serious himself."A ship wants work; and pilots surely *need* work, or who knows what error they may fall into? But, if the pilot will allow—we have been on-port a scant six hours; the errand that brought us here has scarcely been tagged as satisfactorily completed."

"I am, in fact, too eager?" Aelliana asked.

"Naturally so, but—yes."

"What do you propose, then, Copilot?"

"Why, only that we allow the process to work, while good ship and pilots take a well-earned rest."

"Rest!" She gave a small laugh and shook her tawny hair back."I hardly suppose that I can *rest, van'chela.*"

"Well," he said, with a laugh of his own."Perhaps we can think of something else to do."

***

Feinik's lemon-washed dawn was rousting the night when Dollance-Marie returned to her residence. John had let his reserve down, and talked confidingly about what he hoped for their partnership. It had been exhilarating, strange, and made her desire him all the more, this exotic, innocent creature who with one breath agreed to stand publicly as Alabaster's consort, and with the next expressed a wish to live retired. His wistfulness had sparked her genius, and she had offered travel to some less media-ridden locales as something that they might undertake, to broaden their minds.

He had seized upon that, speaking of this world and that—on which subject he was astonishingly well-informed. She was entranced.

Erabeck's security at last alerted them to the hour, and an additional fee brought them to a back door, and what appeared to be a common taxicab. It was in that humble conveyance that Alabaster brought Galahad to his mother's house, and saw him safely inside.

She then directed the cab to her own residence, thereby depriving the media of her presence for more than five hours on the evening. Her ratings-coach would scold her on the morrow, not to mention her head of security, but for tonight—for this morning!—Dollance-Marie cared only for the future, when John would be hers to protect, and to tutor, and to shape into, oh! something that the world had never before seen!

So exalted was her mood that she did not notice the priority message lamp glowing discreetly pale lime on the console by her bed until she had come out of the refreshing room, loosely wrapped in a gossamgay robe, damp black hair flat against her head.

Her first thought on observing the patient light was that here was her ratings-coach, up early, or late to bed, and already scolding, and she was of a mind to leave it until she had slept.

Her second thought was that her ratings-coach never called on the private line; and that, indeed, *that* line was extremely private, being keyed to her mama's code.

A tiny tremor disturbed Dollance-Marie's euphoria.

She sat on the edge of her bed and touched the lime-green panel.

"Good evening, Marie," her mama's voice was so crisp that it seemed she was standing in the room. "I see a steady trending increase in Followers; an increase which our house's profits reflect. I am pleased. I am also pleased with your decision to form young Vernon's initial partnership. He is an appealing boy—pleasantly original. Handle him well and you'll not only please yourself and be the making of him, but you'll have made a strong ally in Vernon.

"Now, if you will be so kind, I have a task for you. We have been approached by the Albion Historical Museum for a display detailing the illustrious history of our bloodline. This is an extremely prestigious opportunity, as I am certain you will immediately grasp, and one which I am pleased to accept.

"Of course, no display of our history would be complete without the inclusion of the Hamptonshire Ruby. I desire that you have it brought to me at once, by courier, and properly insured for guaranteed delivery."

***

As it happened, they had easily hit upon something mutually amusing to pass an hour, and eventually, limbs tangled and pillows in disarray, they drifted companionably into sleep.

Which was rudely interrupted by the persistent chime of the comm, growing louder even as Daav leapt to his feet, spilling yet more pillows. Aelliana dove sideways across the bed to slap the wall unit. She drew a breath and stated with admirable steadiness,"Caylon, *Ride the Luck*."

"This is Gan Bok, security head for Chimra-on-Feinik. Query: Is *Ride the Luck* available to take a package to Albion, immediate and personal pick-up, guaranteed delivery."

"*Ride the Luck* is available at our usual rate," Aelliana said composedly, while her fingers twisted the poor, abused blanket into yet another knot."All of our deliveries are, of course, guaranteed."

"And insured?" demanded Gan Bok.

Insured? Daav frowned, plucked his pants from the confused garments on the floor, and padded out of their quarters.

In the piloting chamber, he touched a toggle on the comm board, directing the ship to trace the call to its source, and brought up a research screen before he skinned into his pants and sat in the copilot's chair.

"What size and weight is the packet?" Aelliana asked, clever woman that she was.

"Eight centimeters by eight centimeters by five centimeters," the security woman said."Point three-five-nine kilograms."

A small thing; and the contact did, indeed, originate from an address said to be the residence of one Dollance-Marie Chimra. He tapped the name into the research screen.

"We will carry it," Aelliana said, which of course she would, mad for work as she was. There followed from Gan Bok a brief direction for their arrival time, and the promise of a transmitted map. The connection was then closed.

Daav, bare back against the cool leather of the copilot's chair, sighed lightly.

Aelliana's step in the hall came simultaneous with the ping that announced receipt of the promised map. Her hand was cool on his shoulder, her breath warm against his ear, as she leaned in to see his board.

"Are we safe, Copilot?"

"It would seem so," he said, waving at his screens. "Fair chance, Pilot."

"Fair chance," she repeated ruefully, "and yet I should have been more careful, so I learn, and run my checks before ever I said *yes*."

"Perhaps."

She laughed lightly, tickling his ear. "What would you have done, had the call proved bogus?"

"Cut it off," he said, touching a fingertip to the appropriate toggle. "It is an unfortunate fact that comm systems sometimes fail to mesh."

"Ah," Aelliana said. "I will recall that. In the meanwhile, I have committed us, and the luck has smiled upon my foolishness Shall you come with me to collect this package?"

"With great pleasure," he said gallantly.

"Meaning that you will in no wise allow me to go by myself. Well, then, if you will, you must have something more to wear, for I see that we are called to a High House."

"As Feinik counts such things," Daav acknowledged, and rose. He turned, and tipped his head.

"Forgive me, Pilot," he said, "but you are wearing my shirt."

"I couldn't find mine," she said composedly, and turned to lead the way back to their quarters. "Come, let us sort ourselves out."

#

Since it was so dainty a packet they were to pick up, he prepared the small satchel, making certain that the transport boxes were coded and functional. Satisfied on that score, he slipped the strap over his shoulder and went to join his pilot on the bridge.

***

Dollance-Marie waited in the public parlor, fully visible to the media. She wore at-home dress that showed her pale skin to best advantage. Her hair was charmingly tousled, as artless as an hour with her stylist could produce.

She had arrived somewhat in advance of the courier pilot's appointment, box in hand. Her mama would wish the whole world to see that the Ruby began its journey well, placed into the hands of a reputable courier, with delivery guaranteed.

She placed the velvet box on the glazed table next to her chair, and tapped the lid, a preemptive silencing of the inevitable wag who would look for ratings by loudly doubting that the Ruby had ever been in the box.

Gemstone on display, Dollance-Marie touched the screen set into the glazed table. The courier articles—guarantee and insurance—had arrived. She perused them leisurely, and set her thumb to the screen in approval.

A gong sounded elsewhere in the house. Dollance-Marie tapped the screen off, closed the velvet box, and settled simulteneously into her chair, and into Alabaster's attitude of cool indifference.

The door was directly across from her chair. It opened.

First through it came Bok, in crisp security grays; her face correctly impassive.

Following, was a small, spare woman in an untailored leather jacket, her hair was an indeterminate color between brown and blond, caught into a tail that hung limply past her shoulders.

Behind the woman came a man somewhat taller than she, also in leather, his figure lean and his face appalling in its lack of finesse. His hair, black, was dressed like the woman's, and he carried a satchel slung by a strap over his shoulder.

"Aelliana Caylon, pilot-owner of packet ship *Ride the Luck*," the woman said, pausing just behind Bok's position to bow, brief and neat. Her voice was admirably clear, and though she had a rather heavy accent, her words were perfectly intelligible.

"We have come," she said, looking into Alabaster's face with eyes that were a surprisingly attractive green,"to take up the package bound for Albion, which we guarantee to deliver."

Alabaster inclined her head coolly, took up the velvet box and gave it to Bok, who in turn held it out to the woman.

"Daav," she said, and the man stepped up, opening the satchel with one hand and extracting a dull brown cube.

"What is that?" Alabaster asked, sharply.

The man looked at her, eyes bright and black.

"We guarantee delivery, intact and on time," he said, his voice deep, and his Terran quick."While the item is in our care, it is protected as we see fit." Perhaps he thumbed a catch. The cube snapped open, and he extended it to Bok, who, after a minute hesitation, placed the velvet box within.

The man snapped the cube shut, and slipped it back into the satchel.

"Thank you," Alabaster said. Alabaster was always gracious to her social inferiors."My mama wishes to have this item with her as soon as possible. Go now, and travel quickly."

The woman bowed again.

"Ms. Chimra," she murmured, and turned so immediately that Bok had to do a rapid two-step to get in front and lead her properly out of the room, the man following both.

Alabaster nodded satisfaction for the media, rose, and left the public parlor by the inner door to the private prep room. It was there that Bok joined her several minutes later.

"Is all well?" Alabaster asked.

"It will go as planned," Bok assured her.

***

The taxi dropped them at the at the main port gate, despite Aelliana's direction that they be left at the service gate, which was nearer to the *Luck's* docking place.

"It's worth my license to do that, Miss," the cabbie said, sounding genuinely regretful. Service gate's for deliveries only. Main gate's for taxi drop-off."

Which of course made it convenient for those on-world who knew the rule.

And for those on-world who wished to relieve two unexceptional pilots of the plain bag casually slung over the shoulder of the taller of the pair.

The attack came within sight of the gate—three masked forms, all of them taller than Daav, rushed out of a side alley, crowding them back into the shadows.

Aelliana swung left under the awning of a vacant store, perilously close to the wall. One of the three followed her, a sharp gleam showing in his low-held hand, a terror that Daav could do nothing to resolve until he had settled the two who had fixed him in their attentions.

He kicked the first where it mattered most to him, spun and came 'round in a crouch, using the second attacker's height against him.

That one was more canny than his mate, now moaning on the ground. He feinted left, vibroblade humming to wicked life in his right hand. Daav, in no mood for finesse, drove forward, swinging the satchel against the armed hand, and driving his head into the man's solar plexus.

His opponent went down, the knife spilling from his hand. He slammed his heel down on it, to be certain; and spun toward Aelliana, incidentally clipping the first man in the head with the satchel, which took care of that problem for the moment.

Aelliana had engaged her opponent. Even as he spun, she came in under the man's longer reach and twisted in a classic *menfri'at* disarm. His weapon arced away, she clasped his arm against hers and twisted, heart-stoppingly graceful.

The man screamed as his arm was dislocated at the shoulder, and a shadow moved in Daav's peripheral vision.

He turned, saw the woman, and the gun rising, her attention all on Aelliana—on Aelliana's back, as she let her man drop, and—

Too far to jump, but not too far to throw. He snatched open the satchel, the cube finding his hand, and he threw, with all his might.

His aim was true. The cube struck the woman's arm; her finger tightened even as the gun jerked, and the pellet discharged into the awning.

She was quick-witted, though, give her that. She wasted no time on her hurt, or her missed target, but leapt for the box, snatching it up with alacrity, and racing away, down the alley.

"Stop, thief!" Aelliana cried, leaping in pursuit.

Daav caught her, hugging her to him with one arm as with the other he sealed the satchel. Peripheral vision showed that a crowd had gathered, watching with interest, doubtless believing the whole thing had been staged.

"You threw the client's package to the person who was *trying to rob us*!" Aelliana's voice was only somewhat muffled by his jacket, her words were, happily, in Liaden.

"I insist upon *at*," he answered in the same language, keeping his voice low."She had a bead on my pilot."

Aelliana stilled."She did?"

"Yes. She did." He did not quite manage to control the shiver; terror rising now that the matter had been dealt with.

Against his side, Aelliana went still. Sighed.

""I propose that we return to our ship, and that we do so quickly, before those who have watched this whole fiasco understand that it is not a bid on the part of one of the low-ranked Leaders for market points."

She moved her shoulders and he released her, looking 'round at the three fallen bravos.

Aelliana's was curled 'round his arm, moaning; his two were still unconscious, though the one who had brought the knife to the game was showing signs of perhaps rousing.

"Pilot?" he murmured.

"Yes," said Aelliana, looking about—at the three damaged, and the minor crowd that had gathered along the street to watch."Let us go, if you please, Daav."

***

The media had followed the pilots of course, Dollance-Marie had depended upon it; had timed their arrival and departure for the slow hours of the early afternoon to insure that the whole transaction would be captured. It was to have been simple—a threat of harm, a relinquishing of the package—who would not relinquish a package that had no value to them, and which was, after all, insured?

No one was to have gotten hurt.

And yet, Dollance-Marie thought, staring at the screen, three people—three men, unknown to her in their masks—had attempted to importune the pilots. To their discomfort.

The pilots had moved quickly, decisively. Dollance-Marie had never seen people move so rapidly and with such focus. The three were disadvantaged before her own operator had achieved position. It was to that operator's credit that she proceeded according to direction, and surely not her fault that the man had thrown so well.

So well, and so wisely. Unbelievably, he hurled the very thing her operator had been sent to retrieve directly to her. She left the gun, grabbed the prize and ran—so the end was achieved, no matter what hash had been made from the means.

But it was peculiar, Dollance-Marie thought, as she turned from the screen, that the man had chosen that *particular* projectile. Of course, the item *was* insured.

And that gave one pause. Dollance-Marie began to wonder if she had perhaps, and unwittingly, employed a brace of rogues. But, no, their references had been clean, ship and pilots legitimately registered, no contracts on-file. She had inspected the records herself, knowing that her mama would do likewise.

Well. Perhaps the man's wits had been addled by the attack, and he had not fully understood what he did. It was no matter. They had done their part; the insurance would cover their loss; her mama would see—as all the world had seen!—what had happened to the Ruby, and all else—

All else would be well.

***

"Now, sir!" Aelliana spun to face him, poised on the balls of her feet there in the center of the piloting chamber."We guaranteed delivery of that packet; the fact that it was insured is quite beside the point!"

Daav eyed her."Is it?" he inquired.

"Yes! Only think, *van'chela*, if it is said 'round port and in the places that pilots go that *Ride the Luck* loses what is entrusted to her for safekeeping, and fails of her guarantee. *We will never work again!* Now, we must find that woman, speedily, and buy the package back from her."

"Do you think she will sell?" Daav asked, watching her face with interest.

"Do you think she will not?"

"I think that the point is moot," he answered carefully.

"Moot? How so?"

"If the pilot will grant me a moment, I will explain. Should you not be satisfied at the end of what I say, then I will myself contact the client, the port proctors and the insurance writer."

Aelliana frowned up at him and crossed her arms over her breast. "Very well," she said sternly."Speak."

**

"Opportunists," Gen Bok said, when she brought the transport capsule to the prep room."People with low ratings and few Followers. No doubt that they saw the transaction between yourself and the pilots and thought they had found a way to improve themselves."

"Well!" Dollance-Marie answered,"they very nearly ruined everything. Is Janida badly hurt?"

"She would have it no more than a bruise. I sent her to the medic."

"Good." Dollance-Marie took a deep breath and looked at the plain brown transport capsule.

"All's well that ends well," she said, which was what her mama said, when a plan had run too near to ruin." She pressed her thumb against the lock, coaxed the lid up—

"No!"

The capsule was empty.

"Call them—*Ride the Luck*!" she snapped at Bok, who snatched the comm from her belt, pressed a button, listened—and looked up with a small shake of her head.

"My apologies, Ms. Chimra. *Ride the Luck* has lifted, on a filed course for Albion."

#

John was in the private room—*their room*, as she had come to think of it—before her. Her favorite wine stood breathing on the table, with two glasses set ready. John himself was in dark blue slashed with silver, his collar well open. The silver spiderweb scarf draped loosely 'round his shoulders called attention to his decolletage.

Dollance-Marie stopped just inside the door, her dolor momentarily forgotten as she took in the whole of it.

"I think you may be correct, that your mama will murder you," she said, walking 'round him and affecting not to see the blush that so charmingly warmed his features."But—if you do not falter, I believe it can be the next fashion."

He looked earnestly into her face.

"Do you truly think so?"

"It will need to be managed, but I think we are the equal of the challenge," she said, allowing her self another circuit to admire his person.

"Perhaps, when we're partnered," John said, sounding nervous—and that brought it all back, so strongly that Dollance-Marie made a small, involuntary gasp.

"Marie?" He turned, and, greatly daring, caught her hands. He searched her face."Is there something wrong?"

She swallowed and met his eyes, permitting him to hold her, though it would hurt all the more, when he let her go.

"Yes," she said, calling on Alabaster's cold courage so that she could meet his eyes."My mama called for the Ruby to be sent home to her. I—I tried to keep it for you, John, but it was no use, and now—now I have nothing to give you—"

...to bind him, for some time, at least...

"Nothing to give me?" he repeated, his fingers tightening on hers."But you had offered partnership—was that a joke?"

"A joke? No, never! I want you—"

"And I want you," John interrupted, wantonly."You are my true friend. We can teach each other. We'll travel." A glimmer of a smile touched his sweet mouth."We'll make new fashions. We'll have fun!"

Fun.

Dollance-Marie stared at him.

Fun.

"I can't remember," she said,"the last time I had...fun."

"I can teach you," he said, smiling more widely. He raised her hands, and bent his head, his lips tasting the tips of her fingers.

"John!" She was scandalized; she was on fire."*What* have you been learning?"

He laughed, lowering her hands, which she was not at all certain that she wanted.

"Dane has been tutoring me," he said."I told him I wanted to re-new as often as he and Erin had done."

"That amused him," she said tartly.

"He seemed...intrigued. When will we partner, Marie? My moth-er told me that she has signed her approval."

"Then—then, at your leisure, sir!" she said, years of training com-ing to her rescue in this odd hour."But, John—the Ruby. My promise—"

"You were *very wrong* to promise me something that belongs to your mother," he said, looking adorably stern."That is like stealing and it is wrong. You ought never do it again, Marie. Promise."

She stared at him, between delight and consternation. No one spoke to her—well. Her mama. And her ratings-coach. But she had never permitted any of her former liaisons to speak to her in such a tone.

But, she thought, he was right.

"Marie? If you steal again, I shall be very angry with you."

Angry with her? A thrill ran through her.

"I promise," she said.

"Excellent."

He raised her hands again, but before he bent his head, she slipped free, and tucked both behind her back.

"Marie?" He asked, tentative.

"You had a task before you," she told him."To chose the date of our formal partnership."

He tipped his head.

"You had said, I believe, at my leisure?"

"I had."

"Then I must tell you that Dane and Erin offered themselves as witnesses and co-signatures, and stand at our service at any hour of the day or night."

"They will be at dinner now," she pointed out.

"Nonetheless," John said, with sweet determination;"I will make the call."

***

The Gransella of Hamptonshire sent her own car for them, and two security persons, arms very much in evidence.

When they were ushered into the lady's presence, Aelliana bowed and thanked her for her condescension.

"You served me so well at Feinik that it is certainly only Balance that I guard you at Albion," the lady said with a dismissive flutter of long fingers."Leadership is a two-edged knife: On the one hand, we have a record of all that we do or say. On the other hand, we provide opportunity for those who neither Lead nor Follow to engage in un-Rated mischief."

Another flutter of her fingers.

"That is the price that *we* pay; the price we *expect* to pay. To ask those who are not Ranked, and who do not seek to Lead—to ask *yourselves*, for instance, to pay our toll to society—that is not acceptable. Now, what have you brought me?"

Daav stepped forward, opened the satchel and placed the transport capsule in her hand. She opened it, removed the velvet box, and opened it, also.

"Ah..." A sigh, of satisfaction and of reverence."Excellent."

Raising the small box, she turned it so that they could see the contents—a single, large ruby, cut by a master, and flashing crimson lightnings at the room.

"This is what you have brought to me," the Gransella said proudly."One of the greater treasures of my house. Had it been lost..." She allowed the thought to fade with a small shudder, closed the box and looked to Aelliana.

"Such service demands a bonus in addition to your regular fee."

Aelliana bowed, gently.

"If you please," she said."What will serve us more than a bonus is your reference. We are new upon the field, and...and, for this time, fame is as good as cantra."

"Better, for fame will bring you more cantra!" the elder lady stated."It is done. It happens now. Your fee has been released into your ship's account. My car will take you back, and my people will see you to safety. Thank you. You have done a great service for my bloodline. And fame you shall assuredly have. I guarantee it!"

Kin Ties

It was the old dream: Herself, the gun heavy in her hand, Grandfather a weight and a wall at her back. Before her, the man who had coldly slain her mother. He looked as his picture, that Grandfather had her study until she knew every line of his face, and would mistake him for no other pilot, on Casiaport or elsewhere.

In truth, it was not an ill-cast face. One could hardly credit that so clear a countenance belonged to a monster—and yet it was so. Grandfather had taught her.

Indeed, indeed, Ren Zel dea'Judan was every inch a monster, no matter how direct his gaze, or sweetly shaped his mouth. For this man, having murdered Elsu Meriandra Clan Jabun, then wrongly called the attention of the portmaster's office down upon Grandfather's business, an action that had cast Jabun from its rightful place among Casia's High Houses—and then? The Balance for this string of murderous mischief? What was brought down upon the head of Ren Zel dea'Judan for his sins against Clan Jabun, and Grandfather, too?

Why, that he should achieve a berth, and rank, on a merchant ship out of Liad itself, while she and Grandfather, the last of Clan Jabun proud enough to bear the name, lived pinched and retired, with neither associates nor allies to support them.

The root of it all was Ren Zel dea'Judan, and for the wrongs he had visited, unprovoked, upon Jabun, he must die.

That had been Grandfather's judgment, speaking as Delm Jabun.

It was Balance; it was hers to carry and commit, and here he stood before her, trembling as she held the gun, with Grandfather at her back. There would be no failure of her will. She would do her duty. There would, at last, be Balance.

24

...she woke before she pulled the trigger.

She always woke before she pulled the trigger, muscles tight, face wet, stomach roiling.

Carefully, so as not to wake the others, she slid out of bed, opened the window and stepped out onto the catwalk.

***

The hatch came down behind them, locking out the rest of planet, and most particularly Delm Flenik, who desired what benefit an alliance with Korval might yet bring her clan. Ah, yes, the ether rang with her desire. And clashed, discordant, with her caution. She would meet with Korval's emissaries—the silly sister and her irregular lifemate—that much, for profit, she *did* risk. But to extend proper courtesy—to offer a guesting, or even so little as a formal meal with the clan entire? No, Flenik was not so rash as that!

"Never tell me you *wanted* another formal dinner out-clan," Anthora exclaimed, snatching the thought out of his head, as was her wont."Had I not understood you to be entirely bankrupt in your account of polite nothings?"

She spun there in the hallway before him, jeweled pins askew among lively dark curls. He would have blamed this state of sudden charming disorder on the brisk breeze that had assaulted them on the gantry, did he not know his lady rather better than that.

His lady. In unlikely fact, as beautiful and fey as she stood before him, silver eyes smiling in a roguish face, Anthora yos'Galan Clan Korval *was* his lady. His lifemate. Recalling it still took his breath.

"Because we have been together so long," Anthora said, tipping her head.

"Because it seems simultaneously that we have been together since space was born, and have only this moment met."

She laughed."There, now—that's pretty said! Perhaps we should have insisted upon dinner, after all!"

It was his turn to laugh."Should I have made Flenik a like compliment?"

"No, that would never do, would it?" she answered, suddenly serious."Father would have said that we must honor her care for Flenik's reputation and resources."

"And so we ought." Anthora's father had followed his lifemate into the long peace years before Ren Zel dea'Judan had stumbled into her life. As represented by his children, Er Thom yos'Galan had been a man of good sense and stern propriety; and—as a Master Trader was unlikely to be an idiot—a strong force for Korval's continued prominence among Liad's High Houses. The lesson that one must respect a delm's care for the clan was sound, but—

"Flenik cannot hope to keep the alliance a secret from her neighbors," Ren Zel pointed out."If our visit escaped notice, the flow of goods sealed with the Tree-and-Dragon through Flenik's warehouses surely will not—and where stands prudence, then?"

"Where it has always stood, I expect," Anthora said,"somewhere between the shadow and the shade. Recall that our mission is to reaffirm existing ties, nor has Flenik been the most timid we have encountered."

No, there was that, Ren Zel allowed. He had permitted Flenik's disrespect of Anthora to put his temper into disarray.

"Surely the lady might be permitted her private thoughts," Anthora murmured, coming back down the short hall to put her hand on his sleeve."We have grown easy between us, sharing this thought and that until speech becomes cumbersome. But we must recall that

Flenik *showed* no disrespect, and if she failed of an invitation to guest, or to dine, proper courtesy to a trade partner does not demand either."

That was also true. He sighed and walked with her to the piloting chamber. Happily, this visit to Flenik was the last of those their delm had set them; soon, they would be on the way to the clan's new home on the world Surebleak, which he and his lifemate had scarcely seen. It was, indeed, the clan's hasty removal from Liad, in compliance with orders from the Council of Clans, that had made necessary the mission he and Anthora had just accomplished. Korval's outworld trade partners, having heard of their banishment, as had all the galaxy, needed to be assured in person by one of the Line Direct that Korval not only intended to honor long-standing associations and agreements, but *was able* to honor them.

That they had not succeeded in soothing the fears of everyone the delm had bid them visit—well, and how *might* they have dealt with Venari, who had instructed the doorkeeper to deny them, and had the poor child hand out through the hatch an envelope containing contracts of reversion.

Venari the timid, Anthora had dubbed him. The reversions had also revealed a man desperately frightened—of the Council, or of Korval—or, possibly, of both.

It's of no mind," Anthora had said."Val Con will send Shan to mend it, and you know *he* will find success, beloved."

Ren Zel watched his lifemate lean over the co-pilot's board, checking for messages. He sighed again, and loosened the collar of his formal shirt. It would be good, he thought, to exchange finery for a sweater and ship clothes—or leathers, if Anthora fancied dinner on the port this eve.

"Let us dine from supplies," she said, her attention seemingly still on the co-pilot's board."So we may be ready to lift for Casiaport, if Tower finds us an early slot."

Ren Zel froze, fingers at his collar.

"Casiaport," he said, hearing his voice flat with old pain."Surely we will not."

Anthora looked at him over her shoulder, the quick movement dislodging at least one pin; he heard it strike the decking—silver to steel.

"Surely we shall, for Korval has desired it," she answered, raising her eyebrows as if perfect propriety was her nearest kin.

He took a breath."As much as one dislikes to speak ill of the delm's—"

"Oh, *do* by all means speak ill of the delms!" Anthora interrupted him."But I beg you not to waste your genius! Wait until we are with them again, for surely you will find none who will agree with you more!"

It was heart-stopping, to hear one speak so of the delm—of *their* delm. The delm was the face and the voice of the clan. The delm husbanded the clan's resources—those resources including the life of every member of the clan. It was for the delm to order, and the clan member so ordered to provide. Without obedience to the delm—without every clan member striving always for the best good of the clan—all would be chaos and barbarism.

And yet—

"I know that the delm wishes to do honor," Ren Zel, forcing himself to speak evenly."However, I believe that—I believe that, *in this instance* the delm has failed to understand how...difficult it is for those who are not of Korval—those who have—those who have known only one world, one Code—who have not seen so much of odd custom as might a scout, or a soldier, a trader—even a pilot—" He paused, the better to weigh his words. Anthora's levity aside, it *was* the delm of whom he spoke.

Anthora had straightened, and stood watching him seriously from silver eyes, her hands tucked behind her back like a schoolgirl receiving a lesson from her tutor.

She said nothing; the ether conveyed the quality of her waiting. *Patiently* waiting.

Goaded, Ren Zel continued, perhaps, just a little, snappish.

"The delm fails to comprehend that there are those who will turn their face from profit rather than stand against custom. There is *no choice* in this offer Korval desires us to bring to Obrelt. The dead do not return to the world, even to accommodate Korval."

Bang!

It was not an actual explosion that assaulted him, he thought—not that. What struck him was only the manifestation of Anthora's anger on the ether.

"There are no dead men here!" she shouted. Her hair was stirring; he heard more pins strike music from the decking, and drew a breath.

"Beloved, you may say so, and I am dismayed to anger you, yet the truth—"

He scarcely saw her cross the deck. He felt his face taken, not gently, between her two palms, and her lips against his, hard, lewd, and desirous, waking his body with a shout and shiver, his blood coming at once to a boil, and almost he spent himself there and then.

Anthora released him as suddenly as she had snatched him, and stepped back.

"Now," she said, hands on hips, and silver eyes snapping. "Produce me this *dead man*."

"Custom," he answered, his voice thin and breathless. He dragged air deep into his lungs."If you deliver me another such kiss, beloved, well you may produce a dead man."

Her lips quirked, but her eyes remained stormy.

"As you told me the story, your delm diced *against* custom at your death—winning you your license and a two-cantra stake."

"So he did, and very bold he was," Ren Zel answered."But that does not mean Obrelt will—or can—abandon all propriety. We—*they*!—are shopkeepers; their strength—the reason that other clans hire them to keep their books, order their inventory, and manage their staffs—is that they *do* observe every propriety and are nothing out of the way." He took another breath, which he sighed out, suddenly tired and wistful.

"The business and the purpose of the clan was twice wholly disrupted by myself. I would, if I could, allow them their peace and their true course. I will say these things to Korval, and accept whatever comes of it."

"As if Val Con—or Miri!—would lash you to the Tree and lay you three stripes for disobedience," Anthora said, and sighed, herself.

"It shames me," she said softly, and he shivered as her sadness brushed him."Shames me, that I have won such a jewel as you are for myself, and for Korval, with no cost, and no honor paid. If it had been Obrelt that had cast you aside of their own will and spite, I would feel differently. But you were stolen from them, cruelly—"

"The man had lost a daughter," he murmured."The heart of his life. Allow a father grief."

"I allow a father all he might require to comfort him, in such circumstance," Anthora said sharply."But delms are held to higher standards."

There was, Ren Zel thought, no denying that. The delm, indeed, ought to reflect what was best and most honorable of the clan, as a moon, reflecting the glory of its sun. Jabun had used the power and position of his clan to bully and, yes, *steal* from those less moneyed, and lower-placed. Ill-done, the whole of it, and like to have killed one Ren Zel dea'Judan in truth, as well as by custom.

"Allow me," Anthora said softly."Allow me at the least to go to your aunt,

beloved. Allow me to kneel at her feet and thank her from my heart, for the astonishment and the delight that is yourself."

How *that* would please Aunt Chane! Ren Zel thought, with a mixture of horror and humor. To have a child of a High House kneel before her, thodelm of a middling mercantile House based upon an outworld? Every sensibility must rebel! And, yet, how could he ask his lifemate, who shared not only his life, but his soul, to carry any shame or dishonor? And especially for this, which was no more her fault than...his.

He stepped forward and raised his hand, gently, to cup her cheek.

"We will go together," he said."You will say all that you must, respectfully and with restraint, and honor will put an end to shame."

Longing swept through him—hers—chill as a sudden rain, and gone as quickly. Anthora smiled at him, and turned her head to kiss his palm.

"Of course it will," she murmured.

***

"Bad night, Bethy?" Sal asked when they met at the caf.

"The dream, again," she said, low-voice, so Rijmont, just behind her wouldn't hear. Grandfather had taught her that it was not only shameful, but stupid, to show weakness. And, indeed, if it had been Rijmont who had dared to ask after her sleep, she might—no, she *would*—have given him the answer he deserved. Sal, though, was—different. Soon after she had joined the team as an emergency fill-in, he had found her sitting on the catwalk in the dark, chin nestled on arms folded over the rail, feet swinging in the darkness above the repair bay, far below. He'd sat down next to her, hooked his arms over the rail, and let his feet swing, too, and saying nothing at all.

It had occurred to her, after they had sat companionably together for some time, that perhaps he was concerned, lest she was thinking of throwing herself from the catwalk to the bottom of the bay—a considerable distance. Nor would such a fear be entirely beyond his scope; Kunkle's Repair had at that juncture only recently lost a team-member to a fall into the bay, which was how the temp-slot had opened for her.

"A bad dream," she had murmured, to ease him; for Sal of course stood senior to her, and was in addition "floor boss." It was a bad policy, to have a supervisor concerned of one's fitness for work.

She'd felt him nod, in the dark.

"Know all about bad dreams," he'd said, and said nothing more.

She resettled her chin on her arm, and stared down into the darkness until her eyes grew heavy and her thoughts sluggish. She'd pushed to her feet, then, staggering slightly, and found Sal's hand there to steady her.

"G'night," he'd said."No dreams for either of us,'til morning."

And so it had been, just as he said.

Alas, his dominion over dreams did not extend for more than a night or two, and it transpired that they met often, after the others were abed and long asleep. The catwalk was the usual meeting place, she sometimes finding him there before her. Later, after the team had voted to accept her fully; after she had seen her true name vanish inside the Terran "Bethy"—when she had built some small *melant'i* within the team—then, some few times, on very bad nights—his or hers—they walked out into the Night Port until they found a bakery or other eatery open on dark-license. They talked, on such excursions. She told him of Grandfather, a little, and how he had been cheated of his last cantra by persons who had been his allies, who he had trusted—and how, because of this break of trust, there had been insufficient resources to allow her to go for pilot first class.

He told her of his life before he'd come to Casiaport. He'd lost kin on his home world, in an repair accident. The *insurance company* had refused to pay on the claim, citing some safety deficiencies at the shop, and so Sal was made homeless, who was already kinless. He had signed on with the Kunkle Franchise, and had assisted in setting up repair yards on two worlds before Casiaport, which was when the Franchise vanished, and the Set-up Team became Kunkle's Repair. Sal had been third senior, then; he, with the two above him in rank, had taken Kunkle as their surname, and filed for a family business license, which Casiaport granted.

Sal was second senior now, behind Nan, Robert having sold back his share and taken a crew berth on a tramp the year before Bethy joined the team.

"Second in line and the bidness in the black," Sal had said during one of their recent Night Port rambles."Time to expand operations, settle in an' get married."

It had been, she thought at the time, a joke, and she smiled. They joked now,; shared commonplaces, and Sal had become...Sal was...

Sal was trustworthy, she told herself. A valued comrade.

Which Rijmont certainly was not.

She received her cereal with a nod of thanks, moved down the caf line, drew tea, and passed out into the larger room, slipping into a table for two near the wall. In a moment, Sal joined her, smiling, though his eyes looked as heavy as hers felt.

"And your own rest?" she asked him.

"Excellent, what there was of it." His smile deepened and her heart constricted, as it came to her that Sal might *not* have been joking, and that a bed-friend might be the reason for both the excellence of his sleep and its brevity.

And what was it to her, she thought in the next heartbeat, if Sal should have a bed-friend—or a dozen such! He was a well-looking man, though Terran, and there was a subtle strength in his manner which she thought must recommend him as a lover.

"Can't talk about it—not yet," he said, spooning cereal."It's looking good though, Bethy—better than—well. Once it's firm, you'll be the first to know."

Breakfast, never particularly flavorful, suddenly sat ill on her tongue. Truly, the cook must have burnt the grain. She put the spoon down and sipped her tea, searching for an excuse to rise from table, so that she need hear no more.

"Better have that," Sal said, nodding toward her bowl."Nan's gotta line on a repair upstairs. Waiting on the earnest hitting the account and and ack on the go-ahead. Should be ready by the time we hit the shift. You in a mood to fly?"

Her blood quickened. When was she not in a mood to fly? And, truth told, though her value to the crew lay in her second-class license, it was rare enough that an opportunity to exercise her skill came forward.

"Where?" she asked, picking up her spoon again and attacking the cereal with a will.

"Long orbit."

She smiled.

"Thought you'd like that," he said, with satisfaction.

He put his empty bowl on the tray; she finished her meal in a rush that would have earned a scolding from Grandfather. But—a lift to long orbit! Such adventures did not come to her every day, nor even every relumma! Even Grandfather must have—

She aborted that thought, and looked to Sal.

"Who comes with me?"

"Dorlit, Jon, Marsel, and Kei."

"Not you?" she asked, disappointed, for the crew never misbehaved when Sal was there.

He shook his head. "Gotta stay close," he said, again with a hint of that secret smile.

"Who will be crew boss?" she asked after a moment, as if she had not seen the smile.

"You," he said, and she froze with her cup halfway to the tray.

"*I*?"

He nodded, setting his empty cup aside. "It's time," he said, which she couldn't very well argue, since it lay within his melant'i to decide such things. Still, she was aware of a certain trepidition.

"Dorlit'll back you up," Sal continued, and she breathed easier. Dorlit was sensible; even Rijmont respected her. And, really, the thought came, rumbling in her head like Grandfather's voice—why should she be trepidatious? Was she not Cyrbet Meriandra Clan Jabun, a pilot of the line? It was her destiny to order her lessers.

Undoubtedly this was true, for Jabun Himself had taught her so. Still, she admitted to herself, it was good that Dorlit would be there, as back-up.

"Time to go," Sal said, pushing back his chair."Not good to keep the client waiting."

"No," she agreed, rising."Nor the ship."

***

He had dressed, not in the finery required of one who came as an emissary of Korval, but as a pilot—leather jacket over dark shirt and tough trousers.

Anthora, tousled and fresh from her shower, considered this ensemble with head tipped to a side. He thought that she would make an argument, though the ether displayed no such brewing storm.

After a moment, she nodded.

"Surely, it is neither a shame nor a wonder, that one of Korval should arrive as a pilot," she said calmly."Will you call for a car, love? I'll be another moment, only."

The car, having brought them from the port into the city, now drew to the curb. The back door slid open. Ren Zel touched the intercom, murmuring "Wait" to the driver, before he swung onto the walk, and bent down to offer Anthora his hand.

She did not require his assistance, of course. But she put her hand in his as she rose lightly to his side.

Together, they turned—and it was then that his heart utterly failed him.

Confronting them—was nothing but a short walkway, and a fence, high and white, with a gate set center to the walk. Beyond, one saw the tops of small trees, such as trees grew on Casia, and beyond those a hint of the house, roof line taller than the trees, and the wink of a window, down below.

Obrelt's Clanhouse. He had grown up here—on this street, inside that fence, within the House, protected by clan and kin.

Until neither had protected him, at the last.

His chest constricted, the fence, the gate, the house blurred out of sense, and it was hard to breathe. He *remembered*—he remembered walking out of the gate, down the walk, to the empty street—incompletely healed, grieving, stunned—*alone.*

Cast out.

Nothing.

Dead.

It was true, he thought, breathless: The dead did not live again.

Despite everything Korval might do.

He could not—gods, he *could not* face this. Dead—twice dead—but for the kindness of Terrans, and the meddling of Dragons.

Three times dead, if he could not get air into his lungs, or calm the frenzied pounding of his heart. Perhaps someone spoke; he thought—but there was the roaring in his ears.

Quick or dead, he *was* a pilot—and in his need he reached for a pilot's calming exercise. The familiar discipline shattered on the rocks of his pain, leaving him lost in a disorienting blackness, chest laboring now, and it was desperation, or instinct, that threw his will into the ether, where there was silence, and the weaving of fine golden threads, calming, and...correct—correct beyond logic, or the designs of men, or the principles set out in the Code.

Ineluctable, the weaving stretched as far as he could compass—farther, in space, time, and beyond—with nary a thread out of place, nor any disruption of purpose.

Peace filled him; wit returned. He cast about, as one did in this place, and perceived nearby a complexity of silver and azure, lightly stitched with ebon and scarlet.

So did Anthora manifest in the ether. His lifemate, his soul, she for whom he would do anything—even live, if she required it of him. He felt a wave of tenderness, wrapped her in it, felt her love fill and strengthen him.

It required an active application of will; he opened his eyes once again.

The fence was in repair, he noted coolly, and had recently been painted. The trees and the roof were in good order. He sighed and felt a burden he had not known he had carried fall from his shoulders. Obrelt prospered. Jabun had honored, at least, *those* conditions of Balance. The clan had not foundered into poverty on his account.

He took another breath, felt Anthora's thought touch him, questioning, and nodded.

"Lead," he said softly, "and I will follow. My print no longer opens the gate, and the House may yet recall that I am forbidden."

***

Chane dea'Judan sat in what had become her favorite chair in the solar at the back of the house, reading. She had since her retirement rediscovered the joys of fiction, surprising herself by finding that her taste ran to tales of high adventure and high melant'i, with improbable twists based on obscure points of the Code.

She had been for many years thodelm, Obrelt's *working hand,* as the vernacular had it, as if the delm had not worked ceaselessly for the clan and the well-being of all, until one evening he had simply sat down in his chair during the hour before Prime and declared that he was rather tired.

When she had come to wake him, just a half-dozen minutes before the hour, he had already left clan and kin far behind.

In the solar, Chane sighed over her book. Even in death, Arn Eld left Obrelt's affairs in good order—the nadelm had been working at his side for more than a year and knew the status of every bit of the clan's business. She had stayed with the new delm until it was plain that the child was steady, then stood aside for her own successor, likewise well-trained and able.

Not that her retirement afforded her endless days of reading. An elder of the house taught the youngers, listened to the halflings, counseled the working adults, and commiserated with her age-mates. All that, and there was still time to read in the sun, vicariously tasting adventure.

From behind, there came a small noise, as if someone scuffed uncertain boots on the warm stone floor.

"Yes?"

"Excuse me, Grand-aunt," Den Ton, who at eight years local was standing his first shift as doorkeeper, said breathlessly. "There's a lady—a pilot. She asks for your kind attention."

Her kind attention? Chane frowned slightly, then made her expression serene, lest the child think that he had erred.

"Come to me," she said calmly, and when he had done so, asked gently, "Has the pilot a name?"

"Indeed, she sends her card." He produced it, relatively unrumpled, from his pocket.

Chane glanced down—and blinked; in that first moment, the clan sign was everything that she saw. Tree and Dragon.

She took a breath. And what had Korval to do with Obrelt, save what they had already done? It had been a Korval Master Pilot who had so enraged Jabun that Obrelt must need forfeit not only their sole pilot, but a clan member of strong melant'i, a tolerant brother, an affectionate nephew, giving to the youngers, full of life, blameless—oh, without a doubt, blameless.

...which Korval had known, and having done damage, repaired what they might, taking Obrelt's dead up into their lead trade ship—no less than *Dutiful Passage*—under the hand of that very same Master Pilot, so came the tale from out of the Port.

Alas, that had been the last tale touching them to come out of the Port, and the delm had forbidden her to seek further, for fear, at first, of what further ills Jabun might visit upon Obrelt. Later, when Jabun's fortunes had turned, and Arn Eld had gone beyond care, it was fear for the boy himself that had restrained her, for whatever—if anything—Korval had contrived, it surely would not suffer a stranger's hand upon it.

And it had been so...very...long. Surely, whatever further doom awaited the innocent dead had long since fallen.

"Grand-aunt?" Den Ton asked, his voice uncertain.

Chane swallowed old anger and sorrow, smoothed her face and looked again at the card, now quivering a little in small, uncertain fingers.

Anthora yos'Galan Clan Korval the legend ran. Not the Master Pilot, then. Or, at least, not the *same* Master Pilot.

"She asked first for Obrelt," Den Ton said."But the delm is from House. Then it was you that she asked to see, Grand-aunt."

Chane sighed."The lady perhaps works with an out-of-date book," she said."In the delm's absence, you must offer the thodelm, child. Where have you placed the pilot?"

"I asked them of their kindness to wait in the visitor's parlor," he said, which was perfectly correct."But, Grand-aunt, I *did* say that the thodelm was to House, if she pleased, and she said that she wished to speak a word to Chane dea'Judan, if the House permitted." He swallowed, his cheeks flushing.

"I ought to have gone to Wil Bar in any case, oughtn't I?" he asked, voice trembling.

"When a stranger comes unexpected to the door and asks for one of the clan by name, yes, my child, it is correct to bring the matter to delm or thodelm." She glanced again at the card, took her decision and slipped it from the child's fingers, closing her book as she rose.

Den Ton looked up at her, mouth sightly open."Grand-aunt?"

"I will see the lady," she said quietly. Wil Bar would only have to call her, anyway. After all, the tragedy which bound Obrelt to Korval had happened on her watch.

***

The repair job had gone well, the crew working in harmony and with goodwill. Not a little of that goodwill had to do with the bonus promised by the client, should the business take no more than forty-eight Standard Hours, which deadline they handily met. This was entirely due to Kei's Satchel, which he had insisted on bringing, despite the protests of both Jon and Marsel, both of whom swore that their kits were complete and they needed no such ragtag collection of odds and ends as resided in the Satchel.

Only, the ship under repair had not quite the standard locking mechanisms, and it had seemed that the bonus and the contract, too, would falter on the lack of a particular nut, absent by age from both Marsel's kit and Jon's, but present very near the bottom of Kei's.

That circumstance had seen the job complete an hour before the client's deadline, and the bonus had been transferred with the repair fee before they undocked and began the long spiral in to Casiaport.

She trusted that the lesson was learnt—and was certain of it when Marsel joined Kei in the galley, and asked how he chose the contents of the Satchel.

Later, when they were returned to Kunkle's small yard, and she had locked down the board, herded her crew to the office and signed the job complete with Nan, since Sal was not to hand—after all that was done, she walked cross-port to the Guildhall—the *Liaden* Guildhall—to show her card and file her hours.

"The record will relay from the Terran hall," said the clerk on duty—a man she did not know from previous visits.

"I prefer to come here," she answered, sharply."Is there a problem?"

He stared at the screen for a long moment; the screen where he would see, in addition to her piloting record and Guild information, her name.

"No problem," he said softly, and pulled the card from the reader, offering it to her on the tips of his fingers."Pilot Meriandra."

"Thank you," she said, snatching the precious thing. She turned, her temper unsettled, and looked up by habit, to the ship board.

Kunkle's vessel, being registered to the Terran side of the port of course did not display, but—

"*Korval*, here?" asked one of those nearby who was also perusing the board, perhaps of the room at large.

She frowned and stared up at the board on the tradeship side, thinking that it was come at last and again, as it had once before—*Dutiful Passage*, which had rewarded the enemy of her clan. Her heart began to beat faster, her hands curling into fists.

"Courier," someone else said, and her eyes jumped, found the name in the middle of the third column—*Dragon Song*—and the name of the pilot who sat as first.

Ren Zel dea'Judan.

***

Chane dismissed Den Ton to the doorkeeper's station and continued alone to the visitor's parlor. She paused a moment outside of the closed door to compose herself and to still a sudden qualm upon the realization that the costume she wore was more suited to the comfort of reading in the solar than greeting High House guests.

Well, she thought, smoothing her sleeves, if Korval *would* call unannounced, demanding speech with one of the clan, then Korval could take what was found—and well it was that she had not been working the garden this noon!

One more deep breath to center herself, then she slid the door aside stepped through.

At first glance, the parlor was empty—second glance found two evenly matched silhouettes against the sun-filled window through which the pilots doubtless admired the small garden planted just outside for the pleasure of those who waited.

Pilots. Chane hesitated, then recalled that the boy had said he had put *them* in the visitor's parlor.

Even as she recalled it, one of the two turned, and came forward into the less dazzling center of the room, where she paused, and bowed.

Deeply.

Chane had been schooled in the forms; Casia might be an outworld, but that did not mean the Code or proper manners were lost.

Having thus been properly and thoroughly schooled, Chane recognized that the bow was of one acknowledging a debt too great to Balance.

Precisely, in fact, the bow she had been about to offer the lady who was now straightening.

"Anthora yos'Galan Clan Korval," the lady stated, in a voice like rich, dark velvet. She gave Chane her whole face, a bit wide in the cheek, with a strong nose, and a chin that was frankly pointed. Not approaching a beauty, this Korval. Which fact one entirely forgot upon meeting her wide silver eyes. Eyes and face were solemn, for all the world as if the lady were an erring halfling awaiting her elder's judgment.

Her elder, in the meanwhile, recalled her own manners, and bowed, not as she had intended, but a civil welcome to the House, and said, gently,"Chane dea'Judan Clan Obrelt."

She straightened."How may I serve you, Anthora yos'Galan Clan Korval?"

The eyes smiled.

"To serve *me*," she said,"you need only greet my lifemate, and, of your very great kindness bestow upon him your kiss."

Her heart constricted painfully and for a moment she thought she might follow Arn Eld, on whom—save one—the burden of the death had lain heaviest. It had been his decision, that the clan could not sacrifice itself entire for the life of only one. His decision, too, to thwart Jabun as much as might be done, within the line and letter of the Code, though he would never after hear praise for it.

"Ren Zel?" she scarcely knew the voice for her own, rough as it was with tears and loss.

The silhouette that had remained at the window turned now, slowly, and walked deliberately forward, stopping at the lady's side, his face set and closed.

It was a man's face she saw, honed by the events of a dozen Standards. A man's eyes, wary, but steady on her own. His shoulders had broadened, filling the jacket he wore with a pilot's easy pride.

A death wounds all it touches, Anthora yos'Galan said—or did she? It seemed that the words had the quality of her own thought, and yet—

This can be Healed.

Of a certainty, Chane thought—can be and *should be* Healed. Arn Eld had taken the worst wound to himself, as a delm must, for the best good of the clan. But the clan—knowing that their safety was bought with the life of one of their own? It had made them timid, that death; it had lessened them and made them aware of how fragile a thing was honor.

"Ren Zel," she said again, and reached to him, her hand shaking as her fingers brushed his cheek. "Child."

Her vision blurred; she felt her fingers caught in a strong grip, and the warm pressure of his lips.

"Aunt Chane," he whispered. "I've missed you so much."

#

It was some few moments before she composed herself sufficiently to allow the child of her heart to seat her, and accepted a handkerchief from his lifemate's hand.

"Shall I call for tea, ma'am?" that lady asked gently, and Chane half-choked a laugh.

"You will terrify the kitchen, if you dare," she said. Ren Zel knelt beside her chair, her hand held between his palms. She blinked the last of the tears away and looked up at Anthora yos'Galan.

"In a moment, I will call for refreshments, and the thodelm, but first, if you will, what it is that *Korval* wants of us?"

"For of course Korval must want something," the lady said ruefully and sank to her knees at Chane's other side. She folded her hands on the arm of the chair and rested her pointed chin on them.

"And yet, as it happens, Korval *does* want something," Ren Zel murmured.

"True enough," the lady agreed, and slanted her eyes whimsically at Chane's face.

Ren Zel, thought his aunt, must find life interesting with such a charming scoundrel at his side. Anthora yos'Galan laughed, merrily, but with no cause that Chane detected. There were rumors, she thought, recalling them now, that the youngest yos'Galan was not quite right in her head...

"You must forgive my lady," Ren Zel murmured."She is from time to time flutter-headed." He glanced at the lady in question."Are you not, beloved?"

"Indeed I am," she answered."I will also allow 'quicker to school than to be schooled.'" She smiled, sweetly.

"You were," Ren Zel prodded softly,"charged by the delm to speak."

"So I was." Anthora yos'Galan sat back on her heels, folded her hands onto her knees like a good, obedient child, and inclined her head gravely.

"I am to say, on behalf of Korval, that Obrelt's loss is three times Korval's gain. Korval therefore seeks Balance between our two clans. That custom does not allow us to sign contract and compensate

Obrelt rightly for its treasure, we are aware. However, Balance may be achieved in other ways, if Obrelt is willing." The lady paused, her head tipped, as if she regarded a written page before her.

"There is," she said, looking to Ren Zel,"a list of arrangements and accomodations that might be made and met, but truly, beloved, I think those best left for Obrelt or for dea'Judan's thodelm."

"I think so, too," he said gently."Aunt Chane? We had heard that the delm was away..."

"So she is." She felt him start, and extended her free hand to stroke his hair."The years bring change," she said softly."Farin is delm now; and Wil Bar stands thodelm."

"And Uncle Arn Eld?" he asked softly.

"Arn Eld embraced peace," she answered, and saw the sweet mouth tighten.

"I had wished," he said, glancing down,"many times I had wished to thank him, for having contrived so well on my behalf. To have managed it so that I kept my license...I would have died in truth, had he not been so bold."

"So I told him, again and again," she said."Perhaps he would have believed you." She took a breath and looked back to Anthora yos'Galan.

"The delm will return by Prime. Will you wait?"

"Gladly," the lady said."And Ren Zel may renew the acquaintance of his kin."

***

She charted a rambling course through the port until the horn sounded for Night Port. The racket of day-side security screens going down, while night-side screens rattled up had roused her from thoughts that had only gotten more tangled the longer she walked.

Night Port. She should go home. Sal would be worried. No, she reminded herself, Sal was not there. Likely, he was engaged more pleasantly, a thought that did nothing to lighten her mood or ease her thoughts. And who was *she*, she thought angrily, to begrudge Sal joy? If she truly valued him as a comrade, she would rejoice in his good fortune.

The crew-room was empty when she pushed the door open. Night Port though it was, it was not so late as that. Her crew had worked hard and on long-shift—they might well have gone upstairs to the dorm. Or they had gone out to celebrate the bonus by drinking it, though surely Dorlit would have—

"Stop that!"

She turned, seeing the door to the back office standing ajar, which it surely should not be, now that Day Port had turned.

There was a confused sound from the dimness beyond the door, as if of boots scuffed on the 'crete floor, a sharp cry and a low grunt.

"Stop it!" the voice came again—"I don't *want* to!"

She threw herself across the room, slamming the door open with one hand, and hitting the light switch with the other.

It was Rijmont she saw first; Rijmont with his back to the door, his weight pinning Lorin against the wall.

"Don't want to, is it?" he snarled."You wanted hard enough just a minute gone!"

"Stop!" Lorin twisted. Rijmont grabbed her chin in his free hand and forcibly tilted her face up, bringing his lips down on hers.

Cyrbet moved, grabbed the man by his shoulder, spun him 'round and slapped his face so hard he staggered back, away from

Lorin. She put herself in front of the girl, and stared at Rijmont, who stared back, the mark of her hand livid on his pale cheek.

"Lorin said no," she said, hearing her voice steady and hard."Leave."

"She said yes, too," he spat, his hands curling into fists."Which one should I believe?"

"You should believe *no*," Lorin shouted, and Cyrbet inclined her head.

"You should believe no," she repeated."Leave, Rijmont," she said again, and added something she had heard Sal say, when tensions ran high,"Take a walk."

"Well, I don't wanna take a walk, *Bethy*. *I* wanna finish what I came in here for, and it ain't no bidness of yours. Who named you crew boss?"

"Sal did," Dorlit's shadow moved in the door. She stepped into the office, Jon, Marsel, and Kei filing in behind her.

"Bethy," she said, with a respectful nod."Need us to do some clean-up?"

***

The thodelm, his cousin Wil Bar, had cannily handled the matter of introductions to the larger House by presenting Anthora yos'Galan Clan Korval and her lifemate. It was, strictly, proper, and gave those who could not meet his eyes leave to look elsewhere.

Among those was his sister Eba, her distress overflowing into tears and a wordless, hasty retreat into the depths of the house.

His eldest sister, Farin, now Obrelt Herself, had no such difficulty. She embraced him, cheek to cheek, as she had sometimes done when he had been more regular, and gave Anthora full honor as Korval's representative. Nor was she behind in the news.

"One hears that the Council banishes Korval from the homeworld," she said, having heard Korval's greeting from Anthora's lips."Forgive me if I seem pert, but this does seem an odd time to be pursuing new alliances. Surely Korval must look first to themselves."

"Korval has always counted allies above cantra," Anthora responded—an answer that had become rote for them both over the course of their journey."And before you protest that we are not allies, ma'am, only consider that Korval and Obrelt are bound together by two events—a death, and a lifemating. We have the opportunity, now, to decide which of those events will inform the future."

He had scarcely to speak at all, it being very quickly settled in principle that Obrelt and Korval would turn their faces together toward the future.

Anthora then presented the delm's list, which Farin received, prudently requesting time to consider the various items in light of the best good of Obrelt. This, his lady readily agreed to, and so they went down to Prime,

Any awkwardness at table was handled simply enough by seating him, with Anthora, at the top, bracketed by delm, thodelm, and Aunt Chane. This left those lower down-table free to talk among themselves, which they did, so the ether told him, with considerable relief.

As Anthora was speaking with Farin and Wil Bar, he applied himself to Aunt Chane. She asked what his life had been like, after he had left Casia, and he truthfully told her that it had been well enough in terms of work and health and friendship.

"How strange, all that came of us wishing to see you properly wed, and the clan enriched by your child," she said pensively."And how much better for all, had we never gone down that road."

"No," Ren Zel said softly, casting a glance into the ether and the orderly waltz of the threads."No, that I cannot allow. Had you not done as you did, I might never have met, and been joined with, my lady." He smiled at her frown and dared to place his hand over hers, where it lay near her plate.

"Indeed, Aunt Chane, you have contrived to make me happy beyond anything I could have known to hope for. I thank you, with all my heart."

***

Marsel and Jon stayed with Lorin, while she, with Dorlit and Kei, took a rather bruised Rijmont to the port proctors. There he would be held until Sal came to arrange his release, or eighteen local hours had elapsed, whichever came first. She had Rijmont's Kunkle ID and pass-keys in her pocket; they would be turned over to Sal when she saw him.

But Sal was still absent when they returned. Nan said, worriedly, that she hadn't thought it would take so long...

"It?" she asked, but Nan only pressed her lips together and shook her head.

"Boss bidness," Dorlit said, around a sudden, wide yawn."I'm beat."

There was a mutter of agreement from those present, and a movement toward the stairs to the dorm. Dorlit stopped with her foot on the bottom step and turned.

"Coming, Bethy?"

She shook her head."I'll wait for Sal."

"See you in the morning, then."

The footsteps faded. She heard the dorm's door cycle, and sighed. It was not conceivable that she would be able to sleep until she had told Sal what had transpired, given over the things from Rijmont's pockets, and heard what he thought of her actions.

That she had done well in the main—she did think so. Though taking one of the crew to the proctors, she thought, carrying a cup of strong tea to the table—bringing the port into a dispute between comrades—perhaps *that* had not been best done. Had there been any room, closet or cubby inside Kunkle's where they might have confined him without the possibility of mischief...but not even Kei could think of such a place.

The more she thought on it, the more it sat ill with her. Kunkle's crew held itself close, meted reward and punishment within the terms agreed upon by the crew. It was as if she had called the proctors into their rooms to restrain Grandfather during one of his tempers. Such a thing would have been improper. Disloyal.

Sighing, she nodded over her cup, half-dreaming and half-remembering...

She remembered Grandfather drilling her with the weapon, striking her when her aim was less than true. Once, the blow had landed more heavily than he had intended; she had fallen and struck her head—and awakened, moments or hours later, in Grandfather's arms, his tears falling hot on her face as he called her over, and over,"Elsu..."

She shook her head, rousing to drink some tea. Out on the port, a horn sounded the half-night.

Sal had still not returned.

It was familiar, this sitting in the dark alone. For a moment, she wondered why—and then she remembered. Before Grandfather had died, when all the rooms except the kitchen, the informal parlor, and the study had been sealed...she had often sat late alone, nodding over a cup of tea, listening to the night-sounds, thinking of death and duty.

That Ren Zel dea'Judan was the author of all the misfortune that had befallen Clan Jabun in the years following her mother's death...by then, she no longer believed. The clan had shrunk to herself and to Grandfather; her elder kin escaping as they could into apprenticeships, alliances, partnerships off-world, where *Jabun* was not a curse, nor *Meriandra* a threat.

After, when Grandfather, too, had gone, leaving his debt and his anger for her to resolve, she took her license, her ring, what coins were hers by right, and walked out of the great, empty house; down to the port, intending to buy passage or find work.

Her coins had not been enough to buy her way off-world in emulation of her cousins; and her second class license did not trump the peril of her name. It was then that she sought the Terran side of the port, and put her name on every available employment list.

So at last she had come to Kunkle's, accepting the comradeship of Terrans; the doubtful camouflage of Bethy.

But she was *not* Bethy—a Terran with neither a past nor melant'i. She was Cyrbet Meriandra Clan Jabun, the last of her clan, and by that fact, the delm. The last possession of the clan, saving herself, its instrument, was a debt. A debt she had never thought she might see Balanced. Until now.

Ren Zel dea'Judan had returned to Casia.

She could redeem everything. No more dishonor. No more nightmares.

She needed only to rise, and to act.

***

In their cabin aboard *Dragon Song*, Ren Zel waked of a sudden, certain that someone had called his name. Anthora lay with her head on his shoulder, her breath deep and regular. He looked into the ether, thinking that she might have inadvertently engaged him into one of her dreams, as had happened once or twice—but it seemed not. Her pattern on the ether was consistent with one who was profoundly asleep, glowing yet with the aftermath of energetically enjoyed lust.

And, yet, it had been so clear. A woman's voice; his name; a sense of—

He laughed, softly. Perhaps, he said to himself, it was you who dreamed yourself awake? Have you become so accustomed to the strange that you fail to consider the commonplace?

Amused, he closed his eyes, settling his cheek against Anthora's hair...

Ren Zel dea'Judan.

This time he opened his eyes to a cabin shimmering with gold.

He blinked, trying to return himself to everyday sight, for surely he needn't see this *now*—when the business with Obrelt was done in all but detail, and Korval, in their wisdom, had begun a healing long delayed.

His daily sight did not return, however, and the threads began to beguile his sense, so that he found himself following this one and that one—and *that* one, which was oddly kinked, hot—feverish.

Ren Zel frowned, reached—and snatched his awareness back to himself. It was not lightly done, to interfere with the threads. Indeed, it were best to have nothing to do with them at all, which he would not, excepting that it was his gift, to be Sighted in this way—and a blessing it was, for it allowed him to share fully with Anthora.

Again, he considered that odd thread, bringing his awareness close, subjecting it to minute study.

The thread pulsed, shedding flakes of gold, showing a core of molten red, like a raw wound.

Ren Zel bit his lip. That was...unnatural. That, he needed to deal with.

Tenderly, he slid Anthora's head from his shoulder to the pillow, and slipped out of bed, rapidly dressing in the glow of golden threads.

"Love?" Anthora muttered sleepily from the bed."What—" Her voice sharpened, no longer sleep-drenched."Ren Zel! Where are you going?"

"I am going out on the port for a moment," he said softly."Sleep, beloved; I'll be back soon."

"Stay!" she cried—a Command, spoken with all the power of an extremely powerful dramliza. He felt the disruption it made in the ether, extended his will and batted it aside as he exited the cabin.

Behind him, Anthora scrambled out of bed and snatched up her clothes. It was a matter of moments only, but he had already descended the gantry by the time she reached the hatch.

Swearing, she ran after, following his signature in the ether.

***

The gun was heavy—heavier even than it was in the dream—but she had no care for that. Was she not Cyrbet Meriandra Clan Jabun? She could bear any burden, save dishonor.

No, that was wrong—no, it *was* right! Grandfather had used to say so, and Grandfather was right. He had been delm, had he not? The delm was always right.

Now, she was delm. And she would also be right.

How noisy it was on the port this evening. She could scarcely hear herself think.

"Bethy!" The voice was familiar—beloved, she admitted it. On this night, she would finally and entirely be truthful with herself. She slowed briefly; he caught up and put his hand on her arm.

"Bethy, hey, I've got something to tell you. Said you'd be the first, didn't I? I'm sorry it took so long to get the papers signed, but—"

"Sal..."

"Are you OK?" He extended a blunt hand and brushed her hair from her brow—tenderly, as if she were a child."Bethy, listen, I've got news. Good news."

"Good news?" She stared, seeing the smile, the *happiness* in him, then turned and resumed walking.

"Hey, aren't you interested?" Sal cried, running after her.

"I am interested—after," she said."Sal, I have a duty. Please, when I return, you will tell me everything—this good news."

He cocked an eyebrow and kept pace with her, his eyes shrewd now.

"Something heavy in that pocket," he noted."You ain't after beaning Rijmont with one of my good wrenches, are you?"

It was a joke. She was expected to laugh. She shook her head."The proctors have Rijmont," she said.

"'bout time. Bethy, you're scaring me," Sal said, and grabbed her arm. Her hand slid out of the pocket, showing the gun.

Sal's fingers tightened. He stopped and pulled her to a stop beside him in a pool of light.

"Sal, let me go."

"Hell I will! Bethy, where're you going? This like that dream you told me about? The one about your grandfather and that burden he put on you? Give me the gun."

"No." She tightened her grip and looked into his face. It would be easy, to give Sal the gun, to let him turn her from this. Bethy might do so. Delm Jabun...could not.

No. She straightened. Delm Jabun *would* not. She would have Balance. For the best good of the clan.

"Release me," she said, as gently as she might."Sal. I have duty."

"Any duty involving a gun needs some close examination," Sal said grimly."Bethy..."

"My name is not Bethy," she told him, sharply now."It is—"

"Cyrbet Meriandra," a man's gentle voice said out of the shadows before them."Clan Jabun."

Sal's grip loosened in surprise. She took advantage of his lapse to pull her arm free.

"Show yourself," she snapped, wrapping both hands around the gun's grip.

The shadows moved, reshaped themselves into a pilot in plain port leathers. His hair was brown, his face calm and comely.

"Ren Zel dea'Judan," he said, with a nod that was courteous, between pilots."Clan Korval."

"If I was you, I'd run," Sal said frankly."Bethy's a little off her head right now."

The pilot smiled, and shook his head; she could feel the weight of his attention on her and squared her shoulders, the better to bear it.

"You called me, perhaps, Pilot?" he asked.

"Perhaps I did," she replied. There was a small sound in the night, and she looked to Ren Zel dea'Judan's right, where another pilot stepped out of the shadows, dark hair stirring about her head, though there was no breeze on-port tonight.

"Ren Zel," she said, her voice soft and strong.

He raised a hand and the other pilot took a breath, folded her hands before her and said nothing more.

So, then. Cyrbet raised her chin and looked into his eyes.

"You killed my mother," she said."My grandfather never forgave you."

"It is a terrible thing," Ren Zel dea'Judan said,"to lose a child."

Cyrbet licked her lips.

"You ruined Clan Jabun," she said, continuing the litany of those things this man had visited upon them."My grandfather hated you for that."

The pilot bowed his head; said nothing.

She raised the gun, slowly, as Grandfather had taught her, until she still practiced what she must do, in her dreams.

"He taught me," she said."He taught me to hate you. He taught me to use this, so that I would, one day, achieve Balance."

The other pilot, the woman, moved sharply, and subsided at once, a hand fisted at her breast; she saw it from the corner of her eye. Ren Zel dea'Judan never looked aside, his face calm, as if the gun had no meaning for him.

"I am here, now," Cyrbet said, going into the High Tongue for the correct phrase,"as Jabun's delm and the instrument of my grandfather's will. He last wish was for Balance with Ren Zel dea'Judan. I hereby fulfill his Balance, for the best good of the clan."

She reversed the gun and extended it to the brown-haired pilot, butt-first.

He stepped forward to receive it; held it with the muzzle pointed toward the ground.

Gently, he bowed.

"Lady, we are in Balance. Your grandfather's will is achieved; Jabun's honor is restored. Let there be peace, and let all wounds heal."

It was done.

Cyrbet felt her knees begin to tremble; felt Sal's hand come under her arm, supporting her.

"All done, now?" he asked, his voice careful.

"All done, now," she agreed, and nodded to Ren Zel dea'Judan and his second.

"Good e'en, Pilots."

"Good e'en," said the woman, coolly.

"Good e'en," said the man. "Sleep well."

"Let's go, Bethy," Sal said, turning her back toward Kunkle's. "You had a long day and a busy night, and you ain't told me yet if you're gonna marry me."

"Did you ask?" she inquired, and the two of them walked away without a backward look.

***

Anthora stepped to his side.

"That," she said, "was extraordinarily dangerous. Please do not expose yourself so, beloved! What should I have done if you had been killed?"

"But how could I have been, when you had extracted the pellets?" he murmured, slipping the gun into his pocket and turning to offer her his arm. "Where are they?"

She extended her fist, opening the fingers one by one to show six pellets lying in her palm—and suddenly laughed.

"All for naught. The young delm was wiser than I guessed."

Ren Zel sighed, looked into an ether stitched with flawless golden threads, and smiled.

About the Authors

Sharon Lee and Steve Miller are the authors of eighteen collaborative novels of science fiction and fantasy, most set in the Liaden Universe® a space opera geography of their own devising. Their latest novel is *Ghost Ship*, published by Baen Books in August 2011. *Dragon Ship* is coming from Baen, in September 2012.

In addition to her work in the Liaden Universe® Sharon has also seen published a contemporary fantasy, *Carousel Tides*, and two mysteries set in the town of Wimsy, Maine.

For a more-or-less-complete bibliography, as well as bios, and a list of upcoming author appearances, please drop by http://www.korval.com

Thank you

for your interest in
and support of
our work
Sharon Lee and Steve Miller